Are you enjoying this au

If so, please leave us a review. We would love to know your creative stories, amazing artwork design, and wonderful suggestions. We are very interested in your feedback to create even better products for you to enjoy in the near future.

Shopping for school supplies can be fun. Go to our page on Amazon http://bit.ly/amazing-notebooks or scan the QR code below to see all of our awesome and creative back to school products!

Thank you very much!

AMAZING NOTEBOOKS

Amazing Notebooks

This Book Belongs to

Aa Bb Cc Dd Ee Ff Gg
Hh Ii Jj Kk Ll Mm Nn
Oo Pp Qq Rr Ss Tt Uu
Vv Ww Xx Yy Zz
0 1 2 3 4 5 6 7 8 9 10

Aa Bb Cc Dd Ee Ff Gg
Hh Ii Jj Kk Ll Mm Nn
Oo Pp Qq Rr Ss Tt Uu
Vv Ww Xx Yy Zz
0 1 2 3 4 5 6 7 8 9 10

Aa Bb Cc Dd

Ee Ff Gg Hh

Ii Jj Kk Ll Mm

Nn Oo Pp Qq

Rr Ss Tt Uu Vv

Ww Xx Yy Zz

1 2 3 4

5 6 7 8

9 10

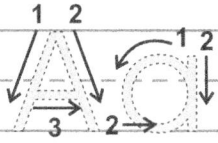 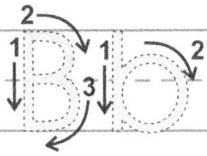 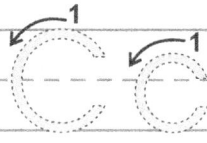 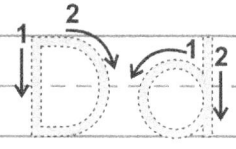

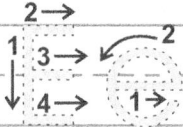 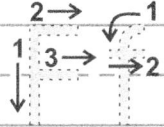 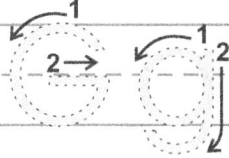 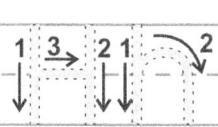

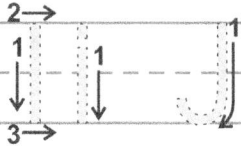 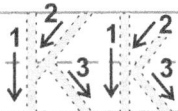 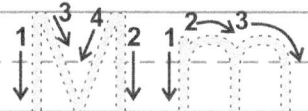

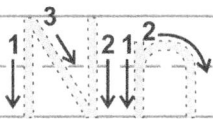 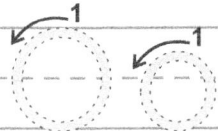 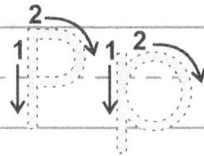 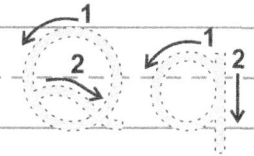

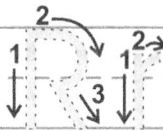 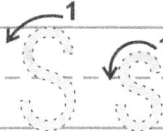 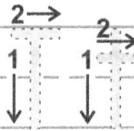  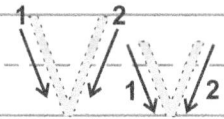

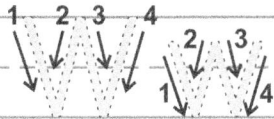 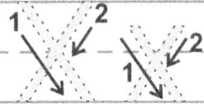 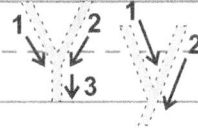 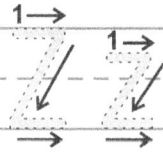

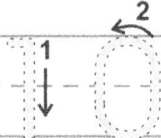

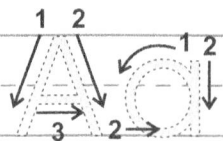 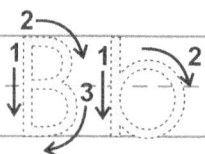 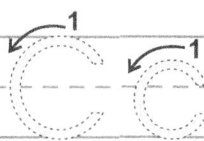 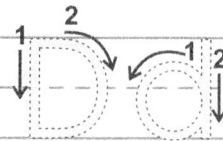

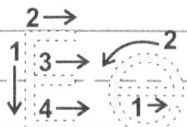 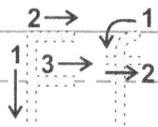 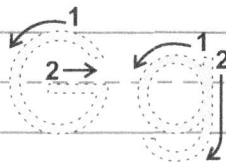 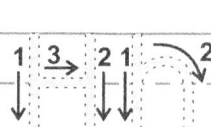

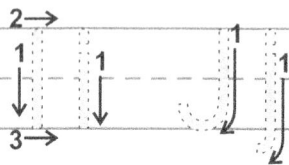 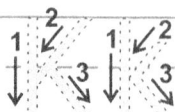 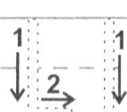 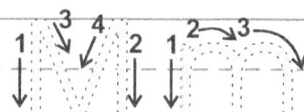

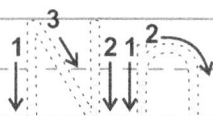 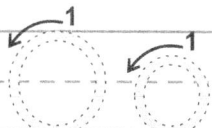 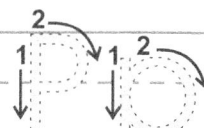 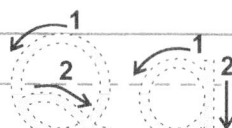

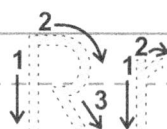 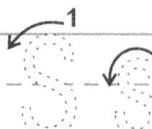 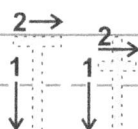  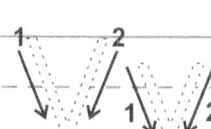

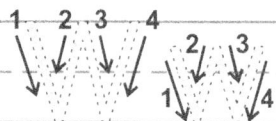 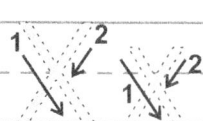 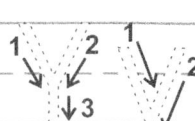 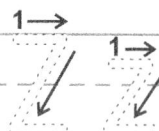

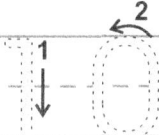

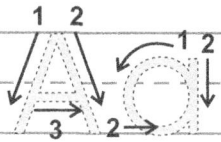 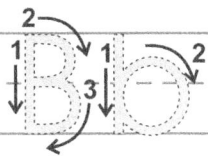 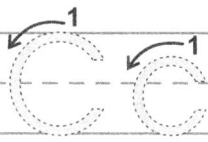 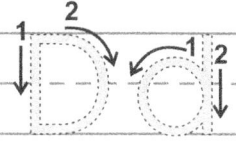

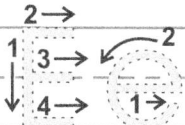 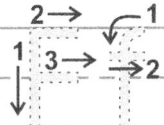 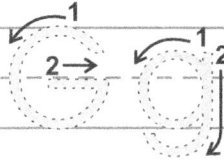 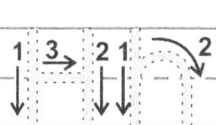

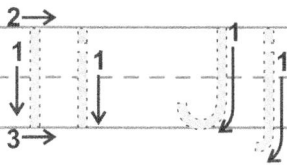 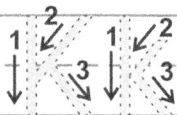 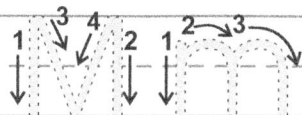

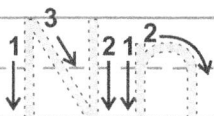 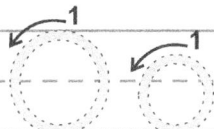 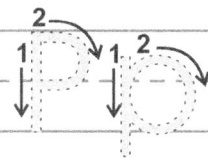 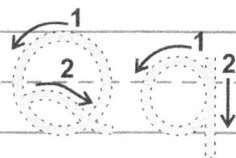

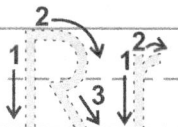 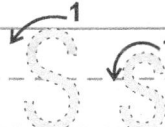 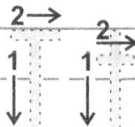 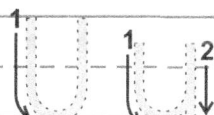 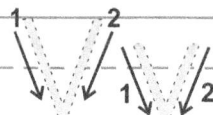

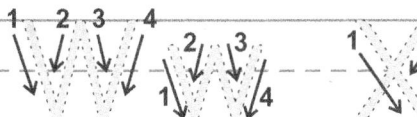 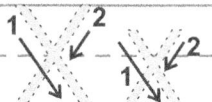 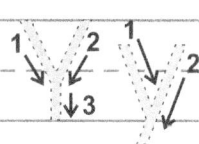 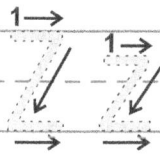

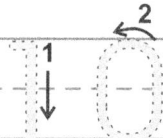

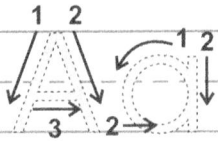 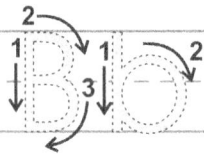 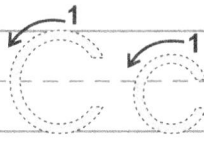 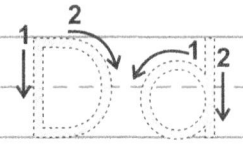

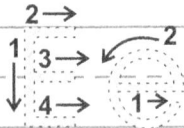 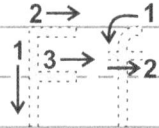 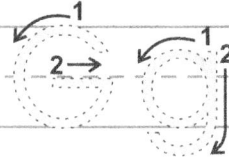 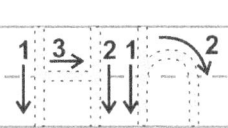

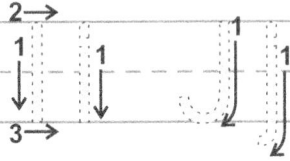 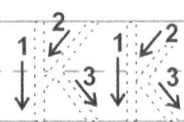  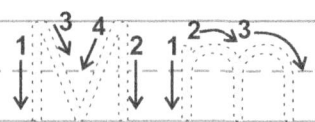

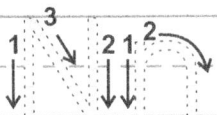 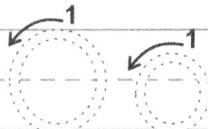 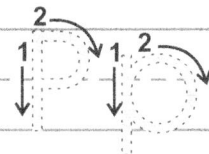 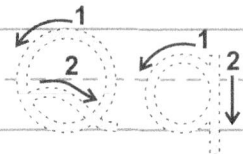

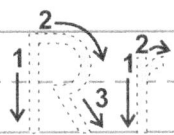 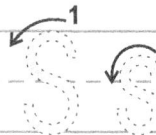 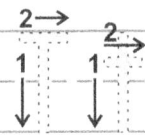 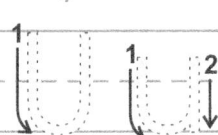 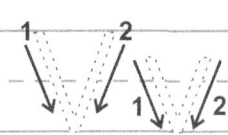

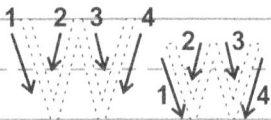 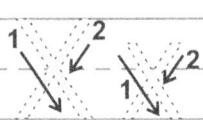 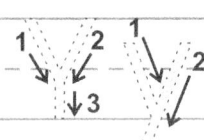 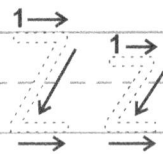

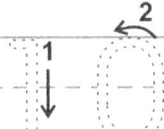

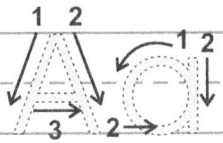 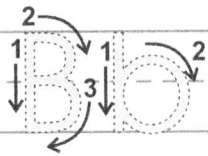 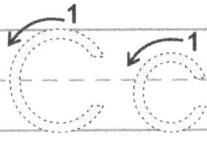 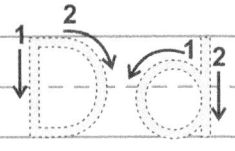

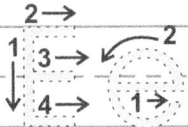 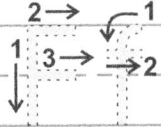 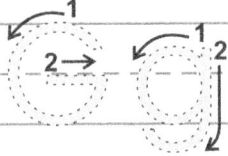 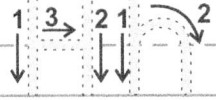

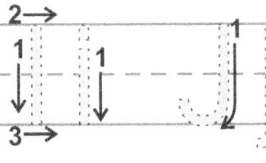 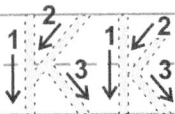 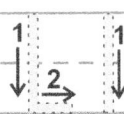 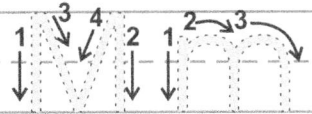

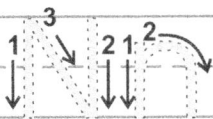 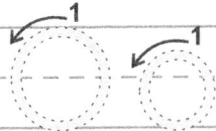 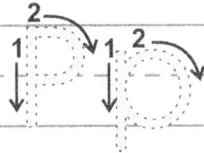 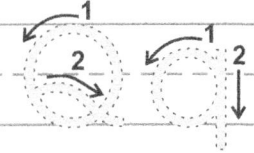

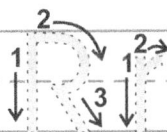 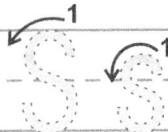 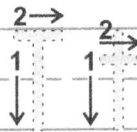 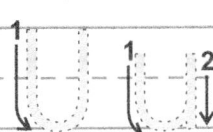 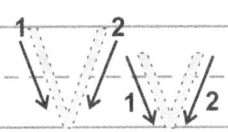

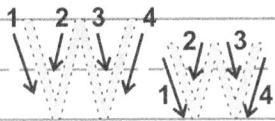 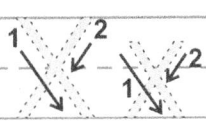 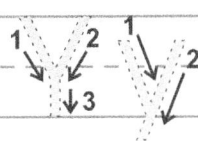 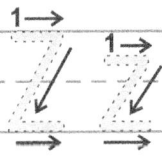

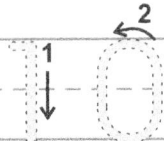

Are you enjoying this awsome book?

If so, please leave us a review. We would love to know your creative stories, amazing artwork design, and wonderful suggestions. We are very interested in your feedback to create even better products for you to enjoy in the near future.

Shopping for school supplies can be fun. Go to our page on Amazon http://bit.ly/amazing-notebooks or scan the QR code below to see all of our awesome and creative back to school products!

Thank you very much!

Amazing Notebooks

Made in the USA
Las Vegas, NV
25 March 2024